For my father, who speaks (almost) every language!
For my mother, who inspired my early love of painting.
For all the travelers, those departing and those arriving …

V. M.

For all the forests of this Earth,
and the birds that live there …
For my parents, who taught me to marvel at them.

É. M.

© for the original French edition: L'Élan vert (Paris, 2008)
Original French title: *Voyage sur un nuage.*

© for the English edition: Prestel Verlag,
Munich · London · New York, 2011

© for reproductions of the works by Marc Chagall:
VG Bild-Kunst, Bonn, 2011. Photography: Artothek, Weilheim.

The Deutsche Nationalbibliothek lists this publication
in the Deutsche Nationalbibliographie; detailed bibliographic information
is available at http://dnb.ddb.de.

Prestel Verlag, Munich
A member of Random House GmbH
www.prestel.com

English translation: Cynthia Hall, Stephanskirchen

Editing: Brad Finger
Layout: Meike Sellier, Eching
Production: Nele Krüger
Printing and binding: Tlačiarne BB, spol. s.r.o.
Printed in Slovakia.

Verlagsgruppe Random House FSC-DEU-0100
The FSC-certified paper *LuxoSamt* is produced
by mill Sappi, Biberist, Schweiz.

ISBN 978-7913-7057-6

Journey on a Cloud

Inspired by a painting by Marc Chagall

Text by Véronique Massenot

Illustrations by Élise Mansot

Prestel

Munich · London · New York

IN A LOVELY CORNER OF THE WORLD, there was a little blue town
of cheerful houses and flowering hills.

This was the place where Zephyr, the mailman,
was born and raised; the place where he learned his trade.
Zephyr knew the town like the back of his hand.

Every morning he traveled the same route:
bringing mail to Flax Street and Cornflower Lane,

to Lapis Lazuli Avenue and Indigo Arcade, and always ending
up in Ultramarine Square.

IN THE EVENING, after work,
Zephyr liked to gaze out of his attic window.
He looked at the sky
along the horizon,
and he saw how the colors changed.

He saw the clouds floating by, playing hide-and-seek with
the setting Sun ... or the rising Moon .

The longer Zephyr stared at the clouds,
the more he saw them change their shapes:
from a giant hen
to a cello,
or from a bearded billy goat
to the Eiffel Tower ...

Zephyr wanted to see
even more of the sky's wonders.
But, alas, his house
was not tall enough!

So he closed his eyes
and let his imagination take him flying ...

THE PEOPLE IN THE BLUE TOWN
were a practical lot. They preferred
to keep their feet on the ground
and their minds on their work.
Daydreaming
          for them was out of the question!

So even though they liked their young
mailman, the townsfolk thought it
a bit odd that his head was always
in the clouds.

Some worried about Zephyr's
thoughts of travel:
"Who would replace Zephyr
if he left our village?"
But others laughed:
"He's never going to leave!
He doesn't have the courage."
"He's a dreamer ... Everyone else
is married, he's the only one who's not!"
"The day Zephyr goes traveling
will be the day my goats learn to read!"
"And the day he gets married,
the angels will descend
from heaven to Earth!
Ha, ha, ha!"

ONE SUMMER EVENING
Zephyr spotted an unusual cloud.
It seemed to dart restlessly from house to house, like a soft,
white flame flickering over the rooftops of the town ...

As the cloud came towards Zephyr's attic window,
the mailman's heart beat faster and faster. He waved to the cloud
as it approached him, anxious to learn its secrets.
"Hello!" Zephyr shouted in greeting.
"Hello!" answered the cloud, somewhat breathlessly.
"What can I do for you?"
"You have traveled all around the world," Zephyr said.
"What is the most beautiful thing you have seen?"
"That's too hard to say," sighed the cloud.

"Climb aboard and see for yourself!"

THE MAILMAN felt his body rise up higher and higher ... At last, he was flying!

The people were astounded,
and they called out from below:
"What are you doing, Zephyr?
Where are you going?"
"I'm traveling to distant lands,"
he answered.
"Are you crazy?" they replied.
"You could get killed!"

"There are so many strange people and so many languages you can't speak!"

"Come back here at once!"

But the cloud had already taken Zephyr
away from his blue home.

The little mailman was now in full flight,
and he couldn't believe his eyes.
What he saw was even more
beautiful than anything
in his dreams.

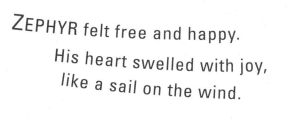

ZEPHYR felt free and happy.
His heart swelled with joy,
like a sail on the wind.

Soon he saw below him a village of bright and glowing yellows.
Dried earth, smooth sand, dusty grass,
and prickly bushes … What a strange sight
for eyes that were used to seeing blue!

The people of the village looked up in wonder …
amazed at this visitor approaching from the sky!
They rushed out of their houses and called out:

"Emoclew! Emoclew!"

But the mailman did not understand them, and he
didn't know how to answer. All he could give them was
his own friendly smile … And then, all at once, a song
of welcome could be heard from below,

Sweeter than honey and more lovely than gold.

NIGHT FELL.
The cloud was soft
and cuddly ...

and Zephyr fell asleep.

"Was I slumbering for long?"
he asked when he awoke.
"Long enough! We have reached
a new land," said the cloud.

Everything around them was bathed iN reD.
Even the inhabitants had red clothes and cheeks.
Having noticed Zephyr, they waved and called out:
„Welcome! Welcome!"
Zephyr smiled and climbed down from the cloud.
„Welcome, traveler!" they repeated. „Come sit with us!"
The red people laughed and spoke a great deal.
They gave Zephyr a friendly welcome and offered him
many delicious things to eat: strange dishes
filled with red tomatoes and spicy red peppers ...
Zephyr's mouth felt stuffed with fire, and his cheeks
glowed as red as the lanterns in the trees. But the friendly
villagers knew what could quench his burning mouth.
So they gave Zephyr an apple as sweet as sugar.

"THIS BREEZE is growing stronger," called the cloud, "it's about to carry me away!," Zephyr perched himself atop his floating friend, and a gust of wind blew them from the red land. Zephyr's blue cap flew off his head and fell down to the village... a gift to the people who had treated him so well.

From far above, Zephyr now saw only a small blue boat merrily bobbing on the waves of the crimson sea.

The air was warm; a storm rumbled in the distance. As it sped across the sky, the cloud grew dark and round, filling the humble mailman with fear.

Soon the storm was upon them, and it sucked them both in. A giant lightening bolt struck the cloud, who roared out in thunderous anger ...
and then wept tears of rain. Zephyr lost hold of his stormy companion, and he fell toward the Earth! Though he hadn't realized it, the mailman had been flying over a vast rain forest. Giant trees held out their leaves to break his fall, and they set him gently upon the ground.

BENEATH THIS ROOF of plants and trees,
Zephyr was safe from the Storm.

But how dark it was here ...

Could there be strange and dangerous animals
hiding in the shadows?

The little mailman felt close to tears.
He thought of his small town
and of his house on Cornflower Street ...
and now his cloud was gone!
How could he get back home?
Suddenly, soft and gentle footsteps
approached. And underneath a
tamarind tree stood the most beautiful girl
Zephyr had ever seen.

As THEIR EYES MET, something special began to happen.
This something was both gentle and strong ...

so beautiful and powerful
that words cannot describe it.

The two strangers looked each other in the eyes,
and the girl slowly reached her hand towards Zephyr,
who gently took it in his.

AND THEIR HEARTS floated away together!
Soon they were both high up in the air … two lovers
at the beginning of a new journey. Would their travels last a whole lifetime?

Both hoped that they would.

When Zephyr returned home with the beautiful girl,
a miracle had changed his small town forever.
For the goats had learned to read, and it seemed
as if the angels were planning a celebration!

Bride and Groom with Eiffel Tower

Marc Chagall

Oil on canvas
150 x 136.5 cm
1938 – 39
Centre Georges-Pompidou,
Musée national d'Art moderne,
Paris (France)

Who was Marc Chagall?

A famous painter who spent most of his life in France. Chagall was born in 1887 in the Jewish neighborhood of Vitebsk, a town that was then part of Russia but is now in Belarus. Vitebsk is surrounded by many blue lakes!

Was he a dreamer?

Too much of one! At least that was the belief of Chagall's parents, who worked hard to support their nine children. But young Marc had a great dream: He wanted to become a painter!

Did he leave home?

In 1910, after taking art lessons in his home town, Chagall continued his studies in Paris. There he got to know other important artists, such as the painters Robert and Sonia Delaunay, Amedeo Modigliani, and Chaim Soutine and the poets Max Jacob and Guillaume Apollinaire.

Did he travel much?

Very much! Chagall traveled through many parts of France—especially the warm, southern regions. In 1941, during the Second World War, he had to flee Europe for the United States. After the war, Chagall's work led him to countries around the world … including Germany, the United Kingdom, and Israel.